Anonymous

The Relative Theory

SALZWASSER
VERLAG

Anonymous

The Relative Theory

Reprint of the original, first published in 1859.

1st Edition 2022 | ISBN: 978-3-37512-220-1

Verlag (Publisher): Salzwasser Verlag GmbH, Zeilweg 44, 60439 Frankfurt, Deutschland
Vertretungsberechtigt (Authorized to represent): E. Roepke, Zeilweg 44, 60439 Frankfurt, Deutschland
Druck (Print): Books on Demand GmbH, In de Tarpen 42, 22848 Norderstedt, Deutschland

THE

RELATIVE THEORY;

IS OR IS NOT

THE BIBLE INFALLIBLE?

AND

THE CRITIC CRITICISED

COMBINED:

OR,

TRUTH VINDICATED & ERROR CONFOUNDED.

" Ye shall know the truth, and the truth shall make you free."

TORONTO, 1859.

THE RELATIVE THEORY,

IS OR IS NOT

THE BIBLE INFALLIBLE?

AND

THE CRITIC CRITICISED

COMBINED:

OR,

TRUTH VINDICATED & ERROR CONFOUNDED.

"You shall know the truth, and the truth shall make you free."

TORONTO, 1859.

PREFACE.

We have written the following by piece-meal, between the hours of our regular vocation, the last piece when we were too much indisposed to attend to it; the other two, without the intention of publication, and *all* in haste. We are not accustomed to writing, and grow better as we proceed. But, we think, we have left it worthy the careful, candid, and serious perusal, and consideration of all, and made it such as to benefit every *honest* enquirer after truth. In each article we have striven to be as clear and plain, as brevity, and good and strong reasoning would permit of. We have sacrificed meter in the attempt at poetry, and the use of a higher class of words and phrases throughout, for this purpose.

We want the unlearned of the schools, to understand as well as the learned—we wish to reach the mass. Nor do we believe in the use of eloquence in controversial writing or speaking. Eloquence addresses itself to, and moves the passions, which becloud the reason, and incapacitate the mind to draw *logical* conclusions. Hence, we should not strive to be eloquent when reasoning, if our object is anything higher than to induce people to fall in with *our* view. Ranting may make converts and bigots, but it does not enlighten the intellect. Witness its fruits everywhere!

Let *truth* be the great high mark,
　At which we all shall aim ;
To the voice of nature ever hark,
　And learn what is *true* fame.

Yours in love and truth,

W. M.

ALL IS BUT ONE:

OR,

THE RELATIVE THEORY.

Whether matter, soul, or mind,
Spirit, God, or nature blind,
All make but a *Unity,*
Which *ever was,* will *ever be.*

Of which change is a property, eternal too,
Which fashions *all things*—as me and you
Who seek the universe too scan,
To account for these things by a plan.

But laws of order as with change,
Have their *co-eternal range ;*
Without which no universe could be,
For each is an *essential property.*

So change, law, order, and this unity,
Exist each, and together as a necessity ;
For it is *impossible* for human thought
To perceive there *ever was,* or *will* be nought.

And too, if something, it must have properties,
As seen, change, law, order, are some of these :
Then why *harp* so much on the word *design,*
Since for it we find no place, no course, no line

These pervade the *stupendous whole,*
And by their power, all things control,
And as with the others, so with the one,
There *never* was a time when *either* begun.

But you say we are foolish, true,
Who differ on this point with you ;
But we ask who did the *Planner* plan ?
Now where are *your* wits—good man ?

Or, how from nothing could something be?
So *now* we have you—don't you see?
And you say without design all would be *chance*,
We have answered, but *order* was in advance.

And is it not as plain to see,
That order is a thing could be?
Aye! would not *disorder* be more strange?
Now, come—give your thoughts a little range.

Break loose your fetters—*be a man*—
Do your *own* thinking, if think you can:
If not, why let your rider still
Be to you whip, spur and will.

By your rider, I mean your priest,
Who sprang from shepherds of the east,
And by his knowledge of *astrology*,
Took advantage of man's credulity.

And have been since the canker worm
That *eats out life's very germ:*
So man has become spiritually dead,
Having *no* respect for his *own* heart or head.

———————

But where is *God?* "God is the soul,"
As Pope has it, of this *One great Whole;*
Whilst *matter* is its outward part,
Head, body, limbs and heart.

God is the *essence* that all pervades,
But in different degrees, in different shades,
God is the *spirit*, the *soul*, the *mind*,
That is a part of *all, as* of mankind.

So part God, part matter, as you see,
We are thus, of the *great One*, an *epitome:*
And if ourselves we scan, both true and well,
We'll have explored *all*, earth, heaven and hell.

———————

And as our *bodies* loose their *identity*,
So will our *spirits*- in *eternity*.
As our bodies return, to help make more,
So will our spirits, to what they were before.

And no *other* theory can I defend,
Since without this *circle*, there would be *end;*
And *nothing* can *end*, as *nothing began:*
But, a *better* theory give if you can.

But if a *beginning end*, there would be an *other*,
An axiom so clear, no *sophistry* can smother,
For instance, a line that has one end, must have two,
Which proves *your* theory of *all things*, *untrue*.

Matter, then, *is* as *immortal* as mind,
For to neither, no *end* can you or I find ;
But the *circle* proves too, as to *condition*,
That *both* are *mortal*, in spite of opposition.

Substance and it's condition must be kept apart,
If to find *truth is* the desire of your heart,
In seeking, *small* truths you must *analyze*,
But then for *great* ones you may *synthasyze*.

Man is not *real*—with your permission—
The *real* is the *substance* and the *condition*.
Man is, but—well, say the *expression*—
Every moment of time changes him in succession.

There is no *right*, no *wrong*, when we're *through seeking*;
Nor mind, nor matter, *absolutely speaking* ;
They are only *comparatively*, *relatively true*,
Like different grades—or, say different hue.

There is but *one great absolute truth* ;
Let it be fixed to the mind of each youth,
The *existence* of that *great Unity*;
That *ever was, now is, and will ever be*.

By not understanding this, the most *learn-d* have gone astray,
And had long spun disputes, about what is clear as day;
Some say there's no matter, some no mind, yet, *as* you see,
There's *both*, or *neither*, as you speak *relative* or *absolutely*.

Though *relatively* speaking, we have them all,
Falsehood, truth, good, evils, great and small,
And a *heaven* to *gain*, and a *hell* to *shun*,
Before our *relative race* is *relatively run*.

Pope once said, "whatever *is, is right*,"
He might as *well* have said there is no night ;
And some say there is no darkness, no cold ;
But all light, all heat ; they are *all* wrong, but bold.

Taking these for *real things* has led them astray,
And *because* the relative theory they did *not obey*;
Whilst they are but *conditions* of these things, so too
Are wrong, darkness and cold, and are equally true.

It's as *true*, that there's *wrong* as that there's *right*,
That there's *cold* and *darkness*, as *heat* and *light*,
All are but *relative*, and *none absolute*.
These statements, I think, the *world can't refute*.

Nor were *any* of these, in a *universal sense*,
Ever *less* or *more*, or will *ever* be *hence*,
For *mark* it is *true*, there is *no annihilation*;
And just as plain and true, too, there is *no creation*.

Pope says, too, "*all partial evil is universal good*;"
"All *discord, harmony* misunderstood."
If by these, he only means, *all* is for the *best*,
He is not so *far* wrong as are the rest.

For though there is evil and good, pleasure and pain,
Misery and bliss, *not one* exists in vain.
Unhappiness or *happiness*, is such by *contrast*,
For *without* unhappiness, no happiness, no bliss at last.

Whatever *matter* doth demonstrate,
The same is *truth* in the *spiritual* state:
And if man *would* but attend to this,
How increase his wisdom, happiness, bliss!

Instance, physical violation and its effect,
The *same* course in the moral you then can detect,
And learn there's *no mercy*—that *law* is but just,
And no longer in *creeds*, but in *goodness* to trust.

It is our *egotism*, that makes us desire
Eternal self-hood to seek, to aspire,
But when we have lived till all selfishness is dead,
It's then we'll blend in with the *great fountain-head*.

E'en *now* we are *individual*, in a very *limited* degree;
I'm not independent of you, nor you of me.
And that you are in *me*, and I am in *you*,
God in us *both*, is as plain as it's true.

But there's a point of dispute between the *good* and the *wise*,
"Does the *soul* remain *separate* after the individual dies?"
The soul's knowledge of it's own *identity*, doth long continue
After the body, it's *less* destructible than bone and sinew.

As you ascend from gross matters to the more sublimated,
The forces become less, by which they can be separated,
And their revolutions less frequent, to whence they emanated,
By *which* duration of body and soul may *be* illustrated.

It's a natural desire of *each human breast*,
To retain a *conscious identity*, *which is a test*
That he *will*; for all unvitiated, *natural desires*,
Are *possible* of *access*, to which the aspirant aspires.

The propensity that looks *beyond man* in trouble,
Is a *proof* there is *something there*, and that *all* is not *bubble*.
Psychology of this consciousness is, *too*, a great test,
And the *phenomena of "spiritualism" set it at rest.*

This long perplexing question, the *free will* of man,"
May now be understood with one single scan.
For practical convenience, or in *comparative degree*,
Not absolute, he may be said to have it, you see.

But as to having free will, *absolutely pure,*
No more than a horse, toad, or stick, I am sure.
A creature of circumstances, yet to them goes to school
And learns, and helps, all other things to rule.

To *each* and *all things he* is dependent;
So are *these* to *him*, no matter how transcendent,
The *consciousness* of his dependant state,
Is the *religious element* primary, and second-rate.

Then *religion is*, for help a want, and a seeking,
Whether by earnest desire, or only just speaking,
Whether from *higher sources*, or from his *brother man*,
He *seeks* it, and *finds* it wherever he can.

Man may be *religious without being good*;
May worship God, man, fire, stone, or wood;
Still *rob* and murder, as they *all have done*,
Since performing ceremonies, rights, or *worship*, begun.

Men perform worship, and follow rights, to *incur favour*,
Which, in time, will be looked upon as *foolish behaviour*.
Nor is love of this religion, the smallest or least part,
Love, goodness, faith, are but helps, to get the *want o*
    the *heart.*

So, too, *original sin*, and man's *regeneration*,

Are points settled easy, by this theory of relation.
To say they are *absolutely real*, is only absurd,
As are all *theological* THEORIES, that I have heard.

Many of the absurdities about *fore-ordination*,
Are founded on ideas of *creator* and *creation ;*
But to the first of this article, a little attention
Will make all these clear, and settle dissension.

All things will come in *order*, though not as designed ;
But as *undeviating laws* and effects will unwind,
And *some time in eternity*, we'll each have our share
Of *all* that is going, but there will be none to spare.

As to *miracles*, the remarks just made, may apply,
But a little farther in their nature, we'll endeavour to pry ;
Their reality we may either deny or affirm,
In accordance with what is meant by the term.

If you mean *law* and *order* were *suspended*, I deny ;
But if only an act by a *highe · power* than man, I comply,
But what's different from us, is affected differently by laws ;
But no more than *we*, can they evade effect and cause.

What would be a miracle on the plane of a horse,
We would *as such*, in no wise endorse ;
And from an oyster, to the *highest* through man,
In what *sense* a *miracle*, shows the relative plan.

From the *highest* individual power of mind,
Down to the *lowest* insect or zoophyte kind,
There's *reciprocal influence* upon feeling or thought,
Sometimes when sought for, but ALWAYS unsought.

That the *link* that's above man, as that below,
Is as *inseperably connected*, must then be so.
Then, that " spiritualism" is true, is a thing that we ought,
And the *true philosopher* will *believe*, without being taught.

So as *philosophers*, Mr. Farada, and all of his kind,
Have proved themselves to be a long way behind.
A *magnetrical media* doth all planes connect,
And the *nearer* the *degrees*, communion the more perfect.

Hamilton says, there is no God as *far* as you *comprehend*.
Cousin, there is none but as *far* as a *knowledge* of him *extend*
These contradictions of these *great* men, though glaring,
Ought not to prevent us, their philosophies sharing.

It's not their *metaphysics* that lead them apart,
It's the want of an *understanding* in *terms* in the start;
As they use the word God, they're both wrong, or both right
But *both* confused by not keeping the *relative theory* in sight.

So all the *great questions* on which great men disagree,
I think may be cleared up by this *relative theory*.
Instead of for *belief, persecution*, and brother slay brother,
Each ought to be *asked*, and *praised* for his view by the other.

This is the *great boundary lines*, the *rock* or the *frame*,
Upon which you may *construct* or fill in that won't be so lame,
A *theology, which we* desire and *do need so much*,
For, *now*, it's *contradiction, confusion, anarchy, as such*.

Now, though in these matters we may disagree,
Still, I hope you will not grow a*ngry* with me ;
You wish the *liberty* to THINK and to *speak*,
The same liberty is *all* that I *seek*.

If I *am* wrong, I *wish* to be right;
My soul craves *light—light—more light ;*
I cannot rest, I cannot stay,
Where light's so scarce, so little day.

I have *scanned your system ;* found it not,
Went on, till, I think, I have it got,
And my desire is, when *truth* I *find*,
To *give* abroad to *all human kind*.

But if *you* have the truth, and *not* I ;
Oh ! *give* to me, or I *pine*, I *die :*
Since by thus giving, as we believe,
You're not impoverished, but the more receive.

But whatever way the case may stand,
Let each extend and lend a *brother's hand :*
Remembering one thing, that *all* do know,
That *our hearts with love should ever glow*.

TORONTO, December, 1858.

THE BIBLE INFALLIBLE?

You say God an infallible being communicated the Bible to man, a fallible being—to *all* through a few individuals as instruments. Then as it has passed through these fallible instruments, how can it have reached us infallible? These individuals were made infallible, first, in understanding God, and next as speakers and writers in communicating it to us; that is in their use of language, (both quite unlikly though) but *language* being imperfect, it would still be fallible to us. God by his holy spirit enables us to understand it—makes us infallible in comprehending its true meaning. Then after all, it is not the *Bible* that is infallible, but on the contrary, it is *fallible*—imperfect, and it is us who are made infallible to understand *it*, the fallible.

In this case then, of what avail is the infallibility of the instruments through which it passed to us, or of what use their services at all. If you were to send a messenger to me with a message, when circumstances were such as to render it necessary for you to come to me yourself after wards, to tell me what that message was, what would be thought of your consistency,—do you think such would be *believed* of *you?*

But is it a *fact* that we are made infallible to understand the Bible—is even this true? evidently not, for different individuals have different understandings of it, which of course shews there is fallibility on the part of some of them at least, if not all; and this difference occurs with those who are equally anxious to get at the truth for its own sake, and are equally honest and willing to comply with the conditions of being thus made infallible to understand, (for we suppose you say this infallibility, or rather the getting of it, is conditional); though here again we would encounter the same difficulty, for without infallibility how are we to be sure we understand the conditions, and so on without end. But does *any individual* understand it to his *perfect* satisfaction? No. then no individual is infallible in understanding it. Does any body of men, such, for instance as the Pope and the major part of his council, inderstand it to its perfect satisfaction? No. then even the Pope and his council, or any body of men is faliable in understanding it. Now if this is true of the first copy written by these few infallible individuals, and in relation to those who could read, what was thus written, what may be said of its infallibility in relation to those who could not read it ; or, what may be said of any, or all of our present translation, in relation *to* all, and of them, in regard to those who cannot read them.

When we have discovered an imperfect link in the chain before passing over three of its links, starting too at its fountain, how many of its countless links would likely be found so, in its dark and mysty coils down to the present time. Yea, is the theme not so rusty and rotten that it will not bear handling ! So say the theologians of the day, by their actions in refusing to come out and defend it, though challenged from all sides.

Though we *have* admitted for argument's sake, the infallibility as writers of the link next to God, what think you of the infallibility of all writers, translators, *printers,* mechanics, &c., &c., that have had to do with it down to the present time? Now even though one were so blind as not to see the imperfections just pointed out, and so absurd as to claim all these last mentioned to be infallible ! surely if he has anything of mind, that raises him above the plane of the lower annimals, when he considers, that for anything to be infallible to us in the sence that it is to be of use to us, it must not be capable of more than one rendering, or of being understood differently by any two or more persons, and when he compares with this the numerous different renderings or meanings that are given it by as many different persons, the hundreds of different translations, all giving each other the lie ; and when he looks at the innumerable sects that have taken different meanings, and *such* meanings too, as to have caused them to commit more butchery, and bloodshed, and crime, since Moses, than any other cause ; as well as to have caused the dearest and nearest relations, not only to break the dearest human ties, but to commit deeds that one would think fiends of hell, (if there are such) not fiendish enough to commit, namely, to slay and murder one another, with cool and deliberate intent, and that too for the *glory* of God ; together with the proceedings of the murderous councils, that have successively contradicted each other from the beginning ; when, I say, he does this, surely he will no longer— can no longer believe in the infallibility of the Bible. Then about it in relation to those, who cannot read it ; but this point is so absurd we have not patience to dwell upon it.

Ask the Mahometan, the Brahmin, the Buddhist, (or even the Jew,) if it be infallible, and each will tell you no ; for they have each their infallible Bible that tells other tales claimed though, to be infallible on *similar* grounds. And why not their decisions be as reliable in regard to your Bible, as yours in regard to theirs ? (they more than double you in numbers, and perhaps are that much older, or more ;) you have no hesitation in pronouncing theirs not only, not infallible, but spurious—concocted schemes of imposition. How much short yours is of this, I leave *you* to judge. He who will not be guided by reason—by *common* sense— hath not common honesty. But why contend, for do not all the learned know, not only that it is not infallible, but that, it, contains spurious and forged passages, as many of them have lately been forced to admit ?

1. John v. 7.—There are three that bear record in Heaven the Father the Word and the Holy Ghost and these three are one, is admitted to be one of this kind by Sir Isaac Newton, Dr. Tomlin, Dr. Marsh, Bishops, Dr. Parson, Dr. Gardner, Dr. Pye Smith &c. &c.,

Now to him who hath common sense and common honesty, we submit the following questions, in order to frame and settle the premises of a syllogism, that we may shew incontrovertably and so plain that the most abtuse mind can see, not only that the Bible is *not* infallible, but that even you do not yourself (or any one who admits the premises,) believe in it's infallibility, for in a true syllogism, if the premises be admitted, the conclusion of course cannot be denied

If equals be added to equals, will the wholes be equal ? Yes. If unequals be added to equals, will the wholes be unequal ? Yes. If an unequal number be added to an equal or any number of equals, will the whole be an unequal number ? Yes. Well then, if an imperfect or fallible part be added to perfect or infallible parts, · ill the whole be fallible ? Yes. Then we have for our major premises whatever is made up of parts (let those parts be what they may steps, links or agencies,) having one or more of its parts fallible, is itself fallible.

Again, has it been clearly shewn in the foregoing that, if *not* all, at least very many,—but if only one it is sufficient for our purpose—of the steps, links, agencies or parts entering into the producing of the Bible to us, are or is fallible ? Yes. This is then the minor premise Of course this minor premise of itself proves all that the syllogism will make clear, for *nothing* is stronger than its weakest part. To illustrate.—If need be you were to cross a precipice or dark abyss, you would not depend for your safety upon a chain, even if it *could* be said of it, that it has strong or *many* strongs links in it, so long as you were aware that it had weak, rotten ones in it, or if it had but one frail link in it, for it would be no stronger, and therefore no safer, than if all its links were equally frail.

THE SYLLOGISM.

Whatever is made up of parts, having one or more of its parts fallible, is itself fallible.

The Bible is made up of parts (in the sense above explained,) one or more of which is or are fallible.

Therefore the Bible is fallible.

But more—Are the conclusions which are drawn from, and founded upon facts demonstrated by science, truths? Yes. Do these conclusions clash with any statements of the Scripture Yes. Then such statements cannot be true. If you cannot deny that two and two make four, you cannot this conclusion; then never again be so false to yourself, as to say you believe the Bible to be infallible. Some of the statements of its different writers contradict each other. Truths cannot contra dict each other, therefore some of these statements cannot be true. The Old and New Testaments teach widely different doctrines, therefore they both cannot teach a true doctrine.

But your quibble may be, that they were given when men were in different states of development; (and by this quibble, like those who, instead of taking an honest, or strait-forward course through life, undertake to shuffle through, often get their feet in the trap, so I think you will; whereas, if you or they had but reflected, you would not have taken the course you have, and would have escaped the difficulty. But you are the two classes that are guided by the impulse of the moment. The man who gained access to you first, and excited your passions most, gained your consent to, and support of his doctrine, and to it you stick, to the exclusion of more reasonable and advanced ones; he does not address your reason and you have not reflected. The other is swayed by apparent presentment of present pleasures, and embraces, to the sacrifice of more lasting happiness. Reflection would have saved you both. If you had taken only what was *reasonable* of this doctrine, you could have afforded to do the same with the next; and if the other had discriminated between those gratifications which do, and those which do not clash with future and greater happiness, he might have enjoyed the latter.) But how does the state of man to which the revelation is given, effect the truthfulness or untruthfulness, the right or wrong of the revelation? surely what has been untrue or wrong since the New Testament days, could not have ever been right. Can right ever become wrong in God's eye?

But then you do not contend that God revealed absolute

truth, or right, but *such* as the people were prepared to receive. This is a great concession : just what we have been contending, that the Bible is not infallible. You *only* say then, that it is true, that it is God's revelation, and that it is the revelation of his *will* to *man*. Then since it has come to this, that *part* of what God has revealed to man is not true; perhaps none of it is, for who knows, but that when man becomes sufficiently advanced, God will make an *other new* revelation, superseding the present new one, and with the anouncement—"behold all things have become new," make it too an *old one.*

We say, by this step you have sliped your neck into the halter, that is, got yourself into a worse position than you were before, which *is*, that *God* revealed a lie ; and the only way for you to get it out, is to turn around, and *yourself* prove that the Bible is not God's revelation at all, for we will not ; we will let you hang for a warning to others against shuffling. But for the sake of others who may have been led astray by you, we would suggest an idea, which is, how much more consistent it would be, to allow ones self to see how plain it is, that if a code of laws, or morals, or theories of faith and worship, are ever changing from less perfect to more perfect, from less consistency to greater consistency, they are *man's inventions, man's* thoughts, theories and plans, and that they become better only as man becomes better, and that man becomes better according to a universal and immutable law of progression.

Civilization advances religion. First teach civilization, next religion, I speak of religion as it is commonly accepted. Religion, correctly defined, is not teachable: it is an inherent propensity of the human mind.

A few words more. Each of these Testaments, in and of itself, teaches different, and opposite doctrines, then all, even of either, is not true. Indeed they appear capable of giving forth so many systems or tunes, according to the skill or tact of the performer, that it would not be unseemly to liken it unto a musical instrument, which may be made to give forth any kind of music.

But to shew that some, even of the most learned, speak of the Bible as being infallible, in the fullest sense of the word, we quote from Archbishop Whately, a celebrated Theologian. "For whatever Scripture declares, the christian is bound to receive, implicitly; however unable to understand it;" 'but to assent to man's framing is wrong.' He speaks of the Bible as if man had nothing to do with it, but as if God drops it into every man's lap, and that each man knows it is God that does it, and as if each can know *what* it "declares," whether he can read it or not.

How absurd! for without man's "framing," there would be no "Scripture." How could there be "Scripture" without language, or without being written &c. &c; and is not language and writing, and all the rest of the instrumental step, or links, "mans' framing?" And even with all its "man. framing," how can the "Scripture declare" anything to those who cannot read without still more of "mans' framing." What gibberish—what prattling for wise men! Then the idea of receiving any thing "implicitly" (that is without investigation, or without the right of questioning, we may suppose him to mean,) "however unable to understand it," is of itsely palpably absurd, and in this connection, is grossly absurd.—By the way, how is the blind and deaf, to know what the "Scripture declares?"

What has been said, is intended to embrace no other idea of, or about the Bible, than its infallibility. We combat this idea, believing it to be at this age, a blight—a curse to Christian nations and people—it impedes their progress in human virtue, and to human happiness.

In the foregoing, there are hundreds of ideas embraced which declare the Bible not to be infallible, a few of which only have been dwelt upon seperately, but more than were absolutely necessary for our purpose. But there are hundreds more that can be brought forward to do the same thing, which are as suggestive too, as those we have chosen, but they are for the most part, such as have been shewn up by others, and very frequently,—indeed all that we have touched upon may have been often before, for aught we know, having read scarcely any works of such a nature. Those we have used do not confine their forces to the Christian's Bible, but show the impossibility, and even the absurdity of the idea, of any one of the bibles or sacred books, of any religion or people being infallible.

But you say, if it happens to be true, *see*, what awaits the unbeliever. Impossibilities never happen. Nothing comes by chance. But suppose it to be true. I can't help my unbelief; for belief is involuntary, and it is as impossible for me to believe the Bible to be infallible as it is for me to believe that God will make it possible for me to hold the Ocean in the hollow of my hand, or to pluck the Sun from his place; for the evidence to me, is about as strong against the possibility of the one, as against the possibility of the other. My soul thirsts for truth, as the plant craves light and heat,—but your theory leaves it yet athirst. But even if belief were a voluntary act of the will or mind, the pure and loving mind, would not, or could not, believe your dogmas, they are so absurd, so gross, so obscene.

Then it seems in the first place, I am to be condemned for not doing what it is impossible for me to do, and in the next place, for being over good. Verily, if I believed in such a God as you *say* you do, and no other, I would feel tempted to do as poor old Job was advised to, "curse God and die!"

As the vine seeks and finds the sturdy and reliable oak, and is satisfied, and flourishes, so my spirit seeks, and if it finds something consistent—the everlasting tree of truth—becomes satisfied, and grows and increases in capacity, for yet more truth, more enjoyments; but if the vine embraces a bundle of straw, it is not satisfied, and soon coils back upon itself, (as the straw rots,) and droops and dies; such would be the fate of the Soul, were it left to depend solely upon your theories; but it is not permitted so to be, for spirit is ever being drawn upward and onward, (as it regards this life at least,) by higher spirits; so that while you are feeding it on straw, and deceiving, and impeding its progress, and lessening its happiness, there is a power that prevents its utter ruin. Many, whilst they think they believe in your dogmas, are comparatively contented and

happy, but their happiness flows from causes they are
ignorant of; sometimes from their own innate goodness,
which is too pure to be scarcely tarnished with the grossness
of their creeds; but as a general law, people will not be
better than their God; and as the Christian's God is in this
Bible, represented to have committed, and encouraged,
and countenanced, the blackest deeds, so we find Christians
doing.

But withall, Christianity has effected much good. When
it was less gross, and when it superseded paganism, it was
a great good. But those whom it came to bless, it remains
to curse; and compared to the light we now demand, it is
a dark mountain, casting its shade, and gloom, and darkness in our pathway—hanging to our necks like a mill-
stone. It has become a superstition. To illustrate, take
for instance the invention and introduction of the common
spinning wheel, and consider what a very great and *posi-
tive* good it must have effected; but suppose this machinery
had remained with us to the exclusion of the vast and mighty
improvements, which have superseded it, would it not in
this wise prove a curse to us? Then imagine the manu-
facturing and vending of this article to have become a mammoth speculation, and that the speculators had a large
amount of capital invested in the same, factories, vending
shops, show rooms, skill, and a peculiar training into a narrow channel, that incapacitated them for other business &c.,
and, that they thought it the most respectable and hon-
ourable business could be; so that in the event of this article being superseded, and there be no more demand for
it, all these things would become of no value, the company
be impoverished, and as a body, die out; and you will have
an illustration of *why*, *a class* is so *desirous* that Christianity should not be superseded. Then imagine this company, most mighty in its power and influence, by means of
its wealth, and brute force, cunning, and ability; and that
to succeed they scruple not, if necessary, to lie, deceive,
rob, and murder; and you will see *why* this class succeed; and see too, that hosts have agreed to accept—agreed
to believe—to escape being burned at the stake, cut up on

the block, tortured by the inquisition, robbed of their lands and houses, cheated, belied, and scandalised ; whilst others join the company, to share the plunder. But in this company, this class, that extends from the Pope down to the commonest ranter, there are, we believe, some who think they are doing for the best, and when they apply their theory to the Heathens, by superseding a still more cramped and imperfect system, they effect good ; and perhaps there are states of mind and society, for which it is peculiarly adapted, just as we might suppose there are people in such conditions as that the spinning wheel, or the thrashing flail, would be more applicable for their purposes than the jinny, or threshing machine.

But while we speak thus of Christianity as a whole—as it has manifested itself to us,—we say that in it are imbodied some great living principles, truths which never can be superseded. But as a whole, it is indigestible to the mind, and when thus taken, impairs its strength, and makes it dispeptic, so that it cannot afterwards digest and be invigorated by its natural food, viz : that which is reasonable ; and hence the morbid state of society ; a state in which it appears to be not capable or willing to receive anything, but what panders to this morbid taste, or is accompanied by the excitement of passion ; as the dispeptic requires unnatural stimulants mixed with his food, and perhaps the stimulants are all that he has felt the effects of, whilst the portions that would have been food to him in a healthy state, pass undigested. Then take advice, and sift the wheat from the chaff, and be really benefited, as well as left capacitated for doing the same on other and all occasions ; and when any one tries to cram you with nonsense, though they do "rap it round, with pomp and darkness till it seems profound," be something like, or I would say, take a lesson from a Brahman, who, when a Christian missionary was trying to explain the theory of God dying for man, exclaimed, "he don't know anything." But I don't say but what there is as glaring nonsense in the Brahman's theory as what he discovered in the Christian's.

"Cast off the pampered bigot slave
Who speaks for hire and pelf,
And teaches that there is no truth
Beyond his creed-bound self."

Now I can imagine the honest reader asking the question. Since it is so clear as to be almost self evident—if not quite so—that the Bible is not infallible, why so many (including as well the learned as the unlearned, the philosopher as the simple-minded, the honest and the dishonest) say they believe it to be so? In the foregoing remarks on Christianity, we have in part answered this question, though somewhat indirectly, and have shown why this professed belief is contended for with such astonishing, and otherwise unaccountable efforts. But believing this question often suggests itself to the honest mind, and when not answered, forms a "stumbling block," to the unpretending, we will endeavour to answer it more fully. The three great causes of this professed belief, in the face of all that is so clear in opposition to it, are *speculation, popularity* and *prejudice* or early impression. Some of each class, the litterate and the illiterate, the reflecting and the unreflecting, are infected by each of these. Some of all these classes are speculators in Christianity (most of the learned class,) who find the idea of the infallibility of the Bible a cardinal point to their success; the fulcrum of the lever power by which they move forward their grand scheme—by which they work their machinery. Then by this and other means the belief became popular, and some of all these classes—most of the unlearned and unreflecting—profess to believe for the sake of popularity; and in this idea of popularity are embraced many petty interests and low consideration, such as belonging to the church or strongest party, to increase their customers in business, to incur the favour and Smiles of greater minds, &c., &c. They float along with the popular professed belief—something on the same principle that dead fish float with the current, or chips on the surface of the water,—to save themselves the labour of steming this current, or thinking for themselves, and from the disagreeableness of being in opposition. Those influenced by these two causes are the dishonest. Some of all these classes—least of the reflecting—are influenced in this belief by early impression, which is the most universal of all causes, as well as the most serious and most difficult to overcome; for "as the bough is bent the tree is inclined." The following quotations will serve to show this point more beautifully than I possibly can.

> " 'Tis granted; and no plainer thing appears,
> Our earliest are our most important years ;
> The mind impressive and soft with ease,
> Imbibes and copies what she hears and sees ;
> And through life's labyrinth holds fast the clue,
> That education gave her, false or true."

And a Saracen says :

> " Our manners, our morals, our fixed belief,
> Are consequences of our place of birth ;
> Born beyond the Ganges I had been a Pagan,
> In France a Christian. I am here a Saracen.
> 'Tis custom forms us all : our parent's hands
> Writes on our hearts the first faint characters,
> Which time retracing deepens into strength
> Which nothing can efface but death or Heaven."

And hence it is, that even many of the learned, and some philosophers, though honest, may be of this belief, having imbibed it as it were from their mother's breast, so that it appears to have become a part of their very being. Yet I cannot bring myself to believe, that any one of thought, and who has made this matter a subject of reflection, can believe in the idea, providing he be an earnest lover and seeker of truth, and has made up his mind to be guided · by it whithersoever it may lead him.

But there is another cause—credulity—which has much influence on the illiterate and weak minded, to whom the language of their priests is, pay us for thinking for you, and we will save you a thousand difficulties, and leave you in possession of the only truth. A Rev. Professor Mattison of New York, in his work, attempting to refute spiritualism and whilst speaking of the investigation of the phenomena, says in effect;—turn your eyes from them, and don't think of these things or anything else, that opposes what we teach you, "and it will save you a thousand difficulties." Then not much wonder that the unfortunate individual, knowing and feeling his own ignorance and weakness, and believing in the superiority of his dictator, and that he is honest, should believe what he is told, even though it were in opposition to his very senses, as well as his reason—examples of which you may find everywhere. We hope this is a sufficiently detailed and satisfactory answer to the question.

These reflections cause us to think of the importance of the subject of youthful education—of what children ought, and what they ought not to be taught. And we think that if Mr. Brown, and Mr. Ryerson, were free themselves from the effects of a wrong system of education—from this prejudice or early impression—and held views founded on their reason and intuition; and had they taken in consideration the philosophy of this early impression, they would not have disagreed on the school question; and thus their time and labour would have been saved from those long spun yarns, that end after all so far short of the truth. To let the mind grow up, free as the breath of Heaven, from all doctrinal points, is the only safe way. When the judgement is formed or matured, let it settle these according to the dictates of its own unperverted perceptions, and inspirations: and then there will grow up a free, a good, and a great people; and the ridiculing, slandering, belying, persecuting and murdering of one another for belief—which is as absurd and unjust, as to persecute me for having a longer or shorter nose than yourself,—will cease, and each will be *pleased* to hear the views of the other. And now in conclusion, I would beg leave to say to you dishonest ones; you who lie and cheat, you leaders, who stick to the people's pockets like leeches, and help to grind the poor to death (in some countries;) you preachers, who ravage and seduce young innocent maidens, (not long ago in the United States, there were thirteen preachers, in three weeks, convicted of seduction ;) that he who deceives others, is deceiving himself; he who cheats and robs others, is cheating and robbing himself most; he who causes to others, however much unhappiness, is laying up for himself still more. That your temporary gratifications in overreaching your neighbours, compared with the consequence of the act to yourselves, may be likened unto one bartering knowledge, which would make him happy here and hereafter, for gold, though he had sufficient of it before to supply him with the necessaries of life : that too, though the absurdities and moonshine of your doctrines, have made you atheists—made you believe there is no God, no hereafter, no judgement; there is a just tribunal before which you will be tried, and from which will come forth a proportionate punishment for all your wrongs. But there will be neither burnning wrath, nor loving mercy to meet you, but simply mild, yet stern *justice.* Every violation has its correction as inseperably attached to it, as effect is to cause—it is cause and effect itself. You see this in the physical laws, and if you will open your eyes but a little wider, you will see it just as clearly in the moral. And to you honest ones, who are yet held fast in your slavish chains of early impression, I would say to you, learn that this condition is the secret of your apparent inability to trust to your senses and reason, and to ascend to freedom; and you will have got over the greatest difficulty in this ascension.

Learn to unlearn what you have learned amiss,
And to try that, by the rule you measure this.
Then you'll find the way to happiness—to bliss,

by first becoming convinced that " knowledge is power to accomplish and to enjoy—that, other things being equal, those who know the most, can accomplish and enjoy the most ; while ignorance, instead of being bliss, is the great cause of human weakness wickedness and woe :" and that nature has " placed in our right hands, obedience with its blessings, and in our left disobedience with its curses, and has endowed us with power to choose or refuse either," (in a certain sense ;) and *then act* upon this belief. "Get wisdom, get understanding," love the truth, learn the truth, and hold it more sacred than all beside. It will enlarge your heart—expand your soul, and make you free! It will make room for a *world* of love to flow in and make you happy. If you would be *happy*, you must *love*; if you would *love*, you must get *wisdom*, learn the truth. Let your Trinity henceforth be VIRTUE! TRUTH! LOVE! Your mediater FAITH! your Heaven HAPPINESS!

"If you wish to live the true life, to be a hero in life's battle, live each day up to your highest ideal, for

> Ever there floats before the real,
> The bright, the beautiful ideal;
> And as to guide the sculptor's hand
> The living forms of beauty stand,
> Till from the rough-hewn marble starts
> A thing of grace in all its parts—
> So, ever stands before the soul,
> A model, beautiful and whole.
> Keep this, each day before thy sight,
> And form the inward man aright.

Live up to this model to-day, and to-morrow you will have a better, a nobler model; and so through life each day will find you a better, holier, happier man. As you scale the mountain of manhood the prospect will enlarge around you, the heavens grów clear above you; the birds will discourse to you sweet music and the happiness of angels will be no stranger to your heart. And when the ripened spirit shall pant for a wider freedom and a sunnier clime, death, the strong deliverer, shall lead you home."

But now,

> "Farewell! and if a better *system's* thine,
> Impart it *frankly*, or make use of mine."

TORONTO, December, 1858.

THE CRITIC CRITICISED.

A Mr. Geikie having delivered a lecture on Emerson, and which lecture he and part of the audience appeared to think a refutation of that gentleman's theories, whilst others thought otherwise ; we think an examination into this lecture, and an impartial investigation of the merits of these two men and their doctrines, as manifested in their two lectures, would tend to settle this difference and effect a good ; and not belonging to the school of either, think we are so far a proper party to undertake the task ; and the love of consistency and truth press us onward to it. Let it be borne in mind that Emerson gave a lecture in the same place a short time before Geikie.

Mr. Geikie's criticism may be considered to have commenced on the evening of Emerson's lecture, when he addressed, the lecturer, extolling the lecture, but expressing a fear, that " a misapprehension of some of the passages might produce a bad effect, by causing some to think less of the Bible than they ought," which said passages were, he said, "something like this, the Bible and Homer, and Shakspere, were what the reader made them—that the light streaming from man himself illuminated the page, otherwise it was comparatively dark." What Mr. Geikie meant by misapprehension we fail to discover, as it is clear that he saw—as every one must have who saw at all—that it was not a misapprehension, but the clear meaning of the passages that would lead to the effect he feared so much. But why did he speak at all ? He surely could not have thought that the lecturer would retract what he had so deliberately said—though it was even Mr. S. C. Geikie who confronted him—but, on the other hand, must have believed that the lecturer would ratify what he had said, (more especially as he knew before, these were Emerson's views,) and make the case which he considered *bad*, worse. And so it was, the lecturer rose with modesty, yet dignity, and in a manner that betokened the same greatness of soul manifested throughout his lecture, and which, therefore, contrasted nobly with Geikie's pompous, yet hectic effort, and said, " I may remark that I am in the habit of regarding the human mind, as the inspired, as our only knowledge of inspiration. The books which we have received—and each of the nations has its sacred books—are all the highest utterances of the human mind. Its religious sentiment expresses its highest utterance, and that is valuable only to a reader in the same mood of mind as that in which the book was written. I think we have almost a proverb in English, that every scripture is to be understood by the same spirit that gave it forth."

But some of the clearer seeing ones would fain have themselves and others believe this a "mystical" reply; not liking, we suppose, the idea that their darling superstition—the infallibility of the Bible—should be denied in plain terms, by one whom they consciously felt to be so much better and greater than themselves. The *Globe* says, " this explanation, somewhat mystical as it was," &c. The real object, however, of the more influential in crying "mystical," was to draw a mist over the minds of the ignorant, (who, they know, will copy after them,) and that they might catch the sound to use as an explanation, or a soother to their conscience, when the question would arise in their minds, how is it, if the Bible be God's inspiration, that so good and wise a man as this, should deny it, and that there is such clear evidence against it ? and it took, for as soon as the sound went out, we heard it echoed by those who were not cunning enough to invent the dodge themselves. The only motive, after all is considered, then, Geikie could have had, as we see it, was to gain popularity ; and certainly, an impudent and unwarantable act ; and as seen, since we have analyzed his remarks, without point or foundation. The *Grumbler* says, an "insane attempt." The *Freeman*, speaking of the act, says, "the intemperate zeal of some rampant biblical," and adds, "how ridiculous that any single individual, no matter what his calling or pretensions, to undertake, in a mixed audience, the responsibility of demanding on behalf of that assemblage, an explanation on a point that his *own* dwarfed and narrow intelligence raised ! The individual, whoever he may be, betrayed very bad manners, worse breeding, and an insufferable amount of insolence. Dr. McCaul administered, we are happy to add, an indirect but telling and caustic rebuke. We hope the zealot has learned a lesson."

If it had been a point that *he* had not already understood, and which *he* wished explained, it would have borne quite a different aspect. We would not dwell so long on so small a matter, but that it is through mens' small acts, we can best understand their motives; and in this we have a clue to Mr. Geikie's motives in his future lecture.

That we may the better understand Mr. Geikie and his lecture, we will first review Emerson's lecture, and through it take a look at himself.

The two greatest elements of goodness, worth, and greatness, are *originality* and *love*. In Emerson's lecture there were manifested many marks of greatness ; but originality and love were its most conspicuous characteristics. These two qualities seem to be possessed by this man in a most extraordinary and apparently unaccountable degree. We believe there is no one living who possesses more of them than he. His manner, his gesture, his style, cannot be traced to any one, they are all his own, they are organic; his very organization and appearance are a sort of original type. But his love is excessive. It is boundless, for it extends to all things animate and inanimate. It is cosmopolitan, no state boundary lines limit its extension. Is universal, it loves all nations, all people—every one, every thing. It pervaded every word he spoke. It shone through his countenance. It glittered in his eye. It is true, no doubt, the lecture was of so high an order, and so spiritual, that the mass—being sunk into the cold materialism of the present state of christianity—could not fully appreciate it. Yet, there was very much in it that *all* could appreciate and be greatly benefitted by.

The subject of the lecture being "The Law of Success," many sayings and illustrations were given, that all must have felt the force of beneficially; but the main rule for success—attending to the impressionability of our nature—we fear many did not appropriate. We were pointed to the fact, that every one having a peculiar organization of his own, is, therefore, fitted for some superiority, and may be successful and great in his sphere, in proportion as he depended upon himself—was organic in what he did and thought.

In short, the advice was, "Man be thyself," and you will be of worth—you will count—but if you will be but an imitator, you will be but a cipher, and instead of enriching civilization with a new product of craft of some kind, or of thought, &c., you give nothing, but weaken what it already possessed. He said, "we impoverish ourselves by giving too much to others—by assuming there are a few great men, and all the rest are little." We should know how to value Socrates, or Plato, or Shakspeare, or the Bible; but not to take *any* as a perfect guide or rule for us, for then our opinions and actions would not be organic—we would be secondary, not primary. " Every man and every woman is a divine possibility."

" We have a central life that puts us in relation to all; we should feel this and not be daunted by things." We were advised to leave off making it our main point to *appear*—to have others think we are what we ought to be merely, and to *make* it our object and our reward, to become something of worth and value. After speaking of an external that learns to read, to trade, to grasp, &c., the lecturer spoke of an inner life, "that loves truth because it is itself true. Loves right, it knows nothing else, and that is always the same, that lives in the great present, and makes the present great, &c.," and said, "Let a man value his talents as it is a door into nature." Let him value the sensibility that receives, that believes, that loves, that dares, that affirms; find the riches of love which possesses that which it adores; the riches of poverty, the height of lowliness, the pursuit of to-day, and in this hour, the age of ages." But we only impoverish and rob the lecture of its greatness by such fragmental quotations. To be appreciated it should be entire.

Touching this matter of making others a standard for ourselves, how numerous and serious are the examples to be found of its impoverishing and deleterious effects. When we look back through past ages, we see here and there have arisen men like great shining lights out of midnight darkness—*original* men,—men who dared to be themselves; others seeing their nobleness, their goodness, their greatness, thinking they would be so too, if they would copy after, not knowing that the secret of their greatness was in being themselves, and that to be great too, they must be original too; they try, but in copying, of course, they fail to a great extent. Being of different size or shape, or temperament, the garment does not fit; but they succeed in forming a clan or sect, that perhaps counts by thousands, no two of which are alike in form, yet each must wear the same coat or shoes as their leader, and a disfigured mass is the result. For some the shoe is too tight in one place, too loose in another, and corns and chafings the result—figurative of men with souls callous on one side, and inflamed on the other. For some it is so tight it cripples them; for others so loose, it comes off and leaves them naked. At first the quality of the garment is kept in view for a while, but soon all idea of quality is disregarded, but the *cut*—the shape! He that would attempt to alter this is no longer fit to live. He is a heretic, a vile wretch; he corrupts morals, poisons the souls of men; he taints the air; society must be freed of the monster; and that his corpse may not poison the earth he must be burned alive!

Thus men become impoverished and wicked by smothering the light within, and looking to the wrong source for that which comes from without. This is an illustration of our point, but it is more, it is one of the faces of christianity.

In the last idea quoted, the lecturer manifested a growth which, we admit ourselves not sufficiently advanced to wholly appreciate—he soared beyond our reach but not out of sight. We feel there is much truth embodied that *we* may put to practical use, and others which are of too high a spiritual order, for our yet comparatively unspiritualised natures to enjoy.

The lecturer's system of reforming society is, not to wait to demolish the mounds of falsehood, but to build temples of truth that will, by their loveliness, attract all men to them, and leave the unsightly masses of error and falsehood to decay and pass away through mere neglect; not the leveling but the exalting principle; not the demonoligical—the scaring principle, but by encouragement, and words of kindness and *love*. But we differ with the lecturer somewhat on this point.

Our plan is to remove the error to make room for the truth ; prepare the soil by destroying the weeds, and removing the rubbish ; but the difference may be owing to the difference in the degrees of our love. Mr. Emerson may believe his seeds of love are sufficiently potent to smother and choke the weeds, and consume the rubbish, and we are not much inclined to dispute him ; yet, we think, both systems have their advantages, but if we could love like Emerson we might see as he does. We are convinced however, that Emerson's system is of the higher order.

We need not speak of the high moral tendency of this lecture, since the lecturer himself was filled with the essence of morality and virtue—*love*.

In proof of the brilliancy of the lecture as a literary, intellectual and eloquent production, we might quote Dr. McCaul's high eulogy upon it Mayor Reed, &c., and the press. The *Freeman* says, "the theories of the lecturer are purely ideal, and we fear will hardly retain realization before the arrival of the milennium." This is *much* for its morality. " In listening, however, to Mr. Emerson, we lose sight of the visionary and follow him captive through the boundless realms of fancy, through the rich parterres of cultivated taste and exquisite imagery— whithersoever he chooses to lead us, without allowing a single pause to stop and admire the sublimity, the grandeur, the simplicity of the variegated variety of the intellectual landscapes which he spreads out before us in rapid succession."

But the *Freeman* finds fault with Emerson for condemning the practice of exhibiting paintings of the crucifixion, &c. He says, it caused him " pain and surprise." Poor fellow ! how we don't sympathize with him. Pity that so elegant a writer should, too, have a bigoted side to his soul. It was the grating of bigotry on the finer senses of his soul in its struggle with truth, which caused the pain. He says, another thing that caused him " pain and surprise," was the applause with which these sentiments were received, &c. Strange the difference in tastes. *This* caused *us* pleasure, and was what we would expect from any enlightened audience, for this sentiment was a part of a beautiful idea given by the lecturer, which required but to be advanced as it was, to gain the consent and approbation of the cultivated taste. In countries where executions for crimes have been frequent, and made public exhibitions of, it has been observed that instead of deterring others, it tended to increase crime, and to lessen the horror of taking life, or loosing it. The idea advanced by the lecturer was, that ghastly and revolting scenes should be kept out of sight, nor should the representations of them be exhibited in rooms, in churches, or any where ; that the unsightly should be covered over—concealed away from view ; and in this we would be only imitating nature, &c. When once our attention is directed to this, how evident it becomes, that this *is* one of nature's teachings.

One pleasing picture catching our attention in our retired moments, may make us better.

Relative to the point of which we have spoken, in connection with Mr. Geikie, the *Globe* reports Dr. McCaul—the president of the meeting—to have said, "He regretted there should have been any mistake as to Mr. Emerson's meaning in one part of his lecture. He had not participated in that idea of Mr. Emerson's meaning, otherwise he would certainly have sympathized warmly with the gentleman who raised the question, which he trusted, however, had now been set at rest." Now, when a lover of consistency, of simple truth, of no shuffling, but straightforward dealing, meets with the like of this, what can he do but expose the shuffler. And though the highest peer in the realm, the monarch on his throne, or our patriarchal father, we would drag him forth without remorse, believing we were not infringing on his rights, for no one dare claim as a *right* to be dishonest, and we have no sympathy with the doctrine, "if you cannot speak well of one, speak not of him at all ;" but we believe it to be our duty, if we know one to be a thief, a liar, or a shuffler, to show him up, nor should the party implicated dare to object to it, since it is one of the great duties of every one to let himself be known.

Though Dr. McCaul belongs to the same school as Geikie, and to that branch of it—preaches or teaches of Divinity as his title implies—which is the cradle of bigotry, superstition and shuffling, yet we look upon him as having a very exalted soul compared to Geikie, and this little shirking or quibbling a much less offense than that committed by Geikie in his criticism on Emerson, as we shall show. In this quotation there are four points which might be considered ; the Dr's. regret that there had been a wrong meaning taken from Emerson's words ; that he did not participate in the mistake ; that if he had he would have sympathized with the individual who took such a meaning ; and that he trusted the question was now set at rest. It is difficult to show this up, for in reality it is all about nothing. All about Geikie's mistake of Emerson's meaning, which was no mistake. The three remaining points rest on the first, which is not itself a reality. But who can doubt that the Dr. took the same meaning from the lecturer as Geikie, viz : that the Bible is not an infallible revelation of God, or to this effect ; and if so, why did he call it a *mistake,* or say he had not participated in it, more especially as the lecturer in his reply reiterated the same idea, expressing himself *more* fully and clearly than at first, as the quotations show.

But on the supposition he had considered Geikie's idea wrong, how could he say with truth and honesty, after hearing the said reply, that he "trusted the question was now set at rest ;" for this implies that the reply of the lecturer contradicted the idea Geikie had taken, or, in other words, the idea that he (the lecturer) had before advanced, which all who heard knows as well as the Dr., and the *reader* may see, was not the fact. As to the Dr's. object and aim, the most we can see in all this, is a shuffling effort to make the audience think, in opposition to facts already stated, that the lecturer did not say anything contradictory to the Bible being what they were taught it was—an infallible Divine revelation—and to do this he necessarily had to imply that this was his own view, which again involves one of two conclusions; that he was dishonest, *or*, that he did not understand the lecturer either in his reply, or in his previous "passages;" but that the latter was not the fact, we have the strongest evidence to convince us, therefore, &c. So turn this matter as you may, look at it from any point of view you will, it shows a dark side. But there is one consideration that may very materially alter all this : which *is*, it the Dr. meant that Geikie's mistake consisted in thinking, that if the people thought the same of the Bible as Emerson implied that he did by the words he used, they would think " less of it than they ought ;" *and* that by not participating in the mistake, he meant that if the people *did* think the same of the Bible as Emerson, they would *not* be thinking less of it than they ought—Emerson's views of the Bible being right. And the more we reflect the more are we convinced that this was really the Dr's. drift. We really hope it was, for it will show he is a freeman—we mean free from the superstitious dogmas, the infallibility of the Bible and its concomitants ; and that the conclusions we have drawn in the other view of the case are wrong, because founded on wrong premises. We do not like to believe that a man of such ability, learning, and position would stoop to shuffling. Taking this view of the matter, the rebuke which the *Freeman* says the Dr. administered to Geikie—as quoted—will become visible : but if this was the Dr's. meaning; had they had called this mystical, instead of Emerson's reply, it would have been like calling things by their right names. We dwell upon this point, for it is important that men of such standing should be understood. And many of them appearing not to believe, or to have learned that it is a duty to let one's self be known, we have to look into them the closer.

MR. GEIKIE'S LECTURE.—We said Mr. Geikie and others appearing to think—we now say professed to think—the lecture a refutation of Emerson's doctrines. Mr. Geikie says, (in reference to some remarks immediately preceding,) "lie a sufficient refutation of Pantheism." He uses the word Pantheism and Emerson's doctrine alternately, as implying the same thing.

Mayor Wilson, who presided, after praising the lecture highly, said, " The doctrine that God was matter and matter God" (as he understood Geikie to make out Emerson's doctrines to be) had been clearly refuted, as had also what was called the " development of system, or the chain of being," doctrines of a " singular" book called the " Vestages of Nature." The lecturer did refer to his, but so slightly, that we were quite unprepared to hear it claimed, it had been refuted, and this too, appeared to be the case with the Mayor, for he forthwith commenced an attempt to do so himself—*and what an attempt!* Did you ever listen to the thrilling tones, and look at the livid actions of some great orator, whose conceptions were so mighty, thoughts and words and actions so sublime, that in hearing and seeing you would seem to almost loose your *own* identity? Did you ever listen to the great artillery of Heaven booming, lou lly, terribly, as if the God of the Universe were speaking, and its lightnings flash as if he were in anger? Or did you ever lie on the table rock of Niagara Falls, and behold and hear, and begin to feel yourself an atom, a speck, or your soul swell to a mountain, from very fullness? Well, if you had, it would have been sure death for you to have seen *this attempt* immediately after, for a *collapse* must have ensued. But to the point. A Rev. Dr. Jennings said he "hoped that his (Geikie's) exposition and refutation of the doctrines held by Emerson, would be sent forth to the world." A Rev. Dr. Lillie also "expressed a strong desire to see the lecture published." Mr. Jennings also said, "when he heard that Emerson had been invited to lecture in Toronto, he regretted it exceedingly, and he thought the fewer there were of these Boston importations, the better it would be for the people. It was unfortunate Mr. Emerson should have expressed such sentiments as he had done, and surprising that he had been left so easily." [These are all from the report of the *Globe* as are most of our quotations.] None will doubt, we presume, Mr. Jenning's sincerity in this expression of regret, *nor* that *all* of his cl iss experience a similar feeling. But why? Jennings and Lillie, of course, would answer, *because* false doctrine. But "dear doctors," is it not granted, and is it not clear, that the nearer and oftener you bring falsehood and truth face to face, the better for truth, and the more falshood will suffer; and that one truth is more than a match for an army of errors. But according to *this* regret and *this* answer, by bringing truth and error to contrast, truth is likely to suffer, and error triumph, and that a whole "city full" of bishops, priests, doctors and deacons—a whole army of generals and officers, as representatives and defenders of the truth, would be likely not to be a match for one layman—one common soldier—as a representative and defender of error. So, if this be the condition of your Divinity, you better *doctor* it a little, it must be extremely ill. As for yourselves—first take a large dose of honesty, give it time to circulate through your whole system, then a dose of general knowledge, this will do for the first course. In our next visit we may extend the prescription. Or in a more classical sense, you teachers of Divinity, if you can't teach a better Divinity than one so weak, teach none. In regard to the next idea, which is in reality embodied in this, it may be said [according to what we have just seen,] that it is not the "being better for the people," that frets them, but the fear that the people might get a taste of something they would relish better than what *they* feed them on, and thereby slacken their custom, and make business dull, and finally destroy it. What has just been said may apply to the third. " It was unfortunate" because it loosened their hold on the people's pockets. But the last one is a little varied. " Surprising that he had been left so easily." Now, *Dr.* you surely blushed when you said this, we saw an insincere smile, but through the *gas* we could not see the blush. We *cannot* believe you were *surprised* at all. Do you think any so short-sighted as not to see that the reason " he was left so *easily*," was that you were all afraid of him ? If you do you deceive yourself. You re-minded us of a number of curs coming out to bark across the path of the generous mastiff which had passed, [but took good care he got out of hearing before doing so,] envious of the admiration bestowed upon him. Mr. Geikie knowing the difference in tastes—that some were dwarfed in mind, and therefore admired dwarfed things, and relying on his success in misrepresenting him, by trying to make it appear his qualities were not really admirable, but the reverse—made this attempt to gain admiration too, and to lessen what had been gained by the other. So you see, Dr., you were not even foremost of the barkers—Geikie commenced first and barked the most.

But to Geikie. First, let us see if this *refutation* talked of and gloried in was real. Let it be understood that we are not undertaking to de-fend all of Emerson's doctrines, or to show that Geikie did not refute *any* of them, [though the latter might be done, he produced no proof against any,] but to confine ourselves more particularly to such as were embodied in his lecture. It is true, in their talk of refutation, they don't speak of Emerson's lecture, but of his opinions and doctrines, on the whole, so those of his lecture must be implied.

Geikie's show of argument appears to consist chiefly in his contrast-ing what *he* called Christianity and Pantheism, or Emerson's doctrines, not being particular about confining himself to what those words imply; but on the one side to attach what he appeared to, and what he thought his hearers would hate most ; and on the other what he liked, or thought the people liked most, and robbing civilization of its claims to clothe it with, and when he did confine himself to its true character, only touched upon some of the least objectionable, and some of its commendable features. This, of course, is no mode of argument, and goes to show he came there, not so much to convince earnest seekers of truth, as to pander to the tastes of those he knew would be there to hear him, or to make another, but greater and more successful attempt at popularity. In reference to what he says is one of Emerson's senti-ments, he says, " We recoil from such a shocking thought." Now, is it likely, that Emerson, a man such as we have just seen him to be, would entertain such a " shocking thought," much less teach it ? That a man so much greater, so much more cultivated, refined, and loving than another, should entertain a thought so " shocking" to that other ? He enumerates many ideas as Emerson's, without giving a shadow of proof that they are, and such as are proved not to be his by his [Emerson's] lecture, and by quotations made by Mr. McLachlan, who lectared in the same place after Geikie. But apart from this, and even supposing he [Geikie] were not inclined to misrepresentation, since [as he acknowledged] he does not understand Emerson's doctrines, these may be but misunderstandings of his own.

He says " Christianity has clothed the savage, given his language form, exchanged his war-club for a spade, sent his child to school," &c. We have read the Christian's Bible, but saw nothing that taught how to make clothes, teach a language, or make a spade, and were under [the impression that these were the legitimate heirs of the arts and sciences: and *so far* from Christianity having a right to claim them, she has been the great opposer of the sciences, and is so *to-day*, as well as of all reform. He says "Christianity makes dissolution only a death-like-sleep, a gentle wafting to immortal life." This is one of the good features of Christianity he touches upon. He insinuates that Emerson's doctrines is in opposition to it ; but dares not venture to say it *is*.

He says Emerson "has no future to which to invite us, or by the prospects of which to cheer us," but "absorption, as when a rain drop falls on the earth." But if this *is* his idea, yet it does not say when this absorption takes place, or that he denies life after "dissolution," but simply that he does not affirm there is. He says Emerson " preaches fate." He taught just the reverse in his lecture. But the great point at issue between the two, and which was made so conspicuous in Emerson's lecture by the circumstances referred to, and which is not only the point which Geikie and his party are the most anxious about, but is in reality the only serious difference between them —the Divine infallibility of the Bible—he totally evaded (as regards undertaking to show Emerson's idea relating thereto, to be wrong, except when he refers to a belief which " gives every man a god," and what he calls a " counterpart to every want of the spirit presented in the Revelation of Jehovah," and says in " these lie a sufficient refutation of Pantheism and vindication of the Scriptures ;") although as seen, he himself had taken objection to it. Is this not a most conclusive evidence that his greatest motive was *not* to oppose error, *not* to vindicate the cause of truth, or what he thought to be error and truth, but *something* much less noble? Then where is the vaunted refutation to be looked for? But he continues his contrast, substituting a little eloquence and some nice poetry [quoted] for evidence, and says, " I set up against all philosophers of Emerson's school, the picture of Cowper's Cottager, and leave you to say whether she or they be the brighter mirror of the highest truth," and gives the picture, which, in the first place, amounts to the idea that some old weaver woman, or any old weaver woman, that knows only one thing, knows what Voltaire did not know, [but that one thing being an error leaves the old woman without knowing *one thing*, and the Frenchman not deficient in *one* thing ;] and, secondly, that *the* or *a* bard, and who is likely to be praised for ages to come, and who has what he prefers, is miserably unhappy; whilst this, or any old weaver woman is exceedingly happy; he receives no reward, she a rich one; he lost, and she safe, [see original.] And now reader *we* " will leave *you* to say" whether this when stripped of its poetry, has any bearing on the question.

So after all, we don't see much in the shape of refutation, of even any of Emerson's opinions, or much to be depended upon as an exposition of them. But if Geikie's lecture deserves any title beside a vague, or, as the *Grumbler* might again call it, an insane attempt at popularity, it is simply a denunciation of " Emerson, his works and opinions."

He commenced his lecture, touching Emerson's history, and saying that after many shiftings he had wandered far, far away from the only truth into outer darkness. Yet Emerson spoke, perhaps as man never spoke, of an inner light—" a central life that puts us in relation to all."

He said Emerson had embraced the extreme of mysticism, vague absurdities and falsehood, " to spread which is the object of his life." Yet Emerson taught in his lecture, the highest morality and virtue, it is possible to conceive of. We should do that respecting the *excellence* of the work and *not* its *acceptableness*, " to confide in one's self and be something of worth and value."

What is it to us, or the world, what a man believes, providing he is of " worth and value," and if he is *not* what of his *belief ?* Geikie denounces Emerson because his belief is not as his own, though he is of a thousand times more worth than himself, and not only that, but his belief is greatly superior. He says, " from Boston, the headquarters of this system, [Pantheism.] Emerson and Theodore Parker, &c., seek to influence the public in any way that offers, " and have so far succeeded for a time, that the Pantheistic tendencies of the age have become a topic," &c.; and in another place he says, " he [Emerson] is known as the representative of ultra-Pantheistic opinions." Yet he told us Emerson was but a faint reflection, the merest imitator of the German school of Pantheists, &c. Such is the manner in which those who do not make truth their greatest aim and object, are apt to confound *themselves*. Nor does this assertion that Emerson is an imitator agree with the *fact* that he is exceedingly *original*. This Mr. Parker, whom, he of course, condemns too, as a teacher of what " our instinctive sense recoils from," is another example of the best, most virtuous, and useful men of our earth—he, too, manifests a degree of love beyond ordinary appreciation or conception.

He says, *they* " have so far succeeded for a time," &c. Vain is your hope, Mr. Geikie, if you expect them to recede before your doctrines *after* " a time." He decries and condemns many of what he denominates the doctrines of the German philosophers, and Carlyle, the Scotchman, too, though admitting they were too mystical for him to

understand, and heaps them, as he traces them down, upon Emerson
as a copyist, because he finds instances where Emerson's ideas have
been similar to the Germans.   On these grounds he might condemn
hundreds unjustly—might say we had copied after Emerson or the
Germans in our *Relative Theory,* because he would find some ideas
there similar to theirs.   But we take this opportunity of stating that
such is not the fact.   We were aware at the time we wrote, that one
or two of the ideas had been given by others, and have learned since
of more, but those that entitle it to the name of the *Relative Theory,* or
the most of them, we are not even now aware of any one else enter-
taining.   Where there is similarity of ideas arrived by men
of thought, such as Emerson, Carlyle, &c., there is proof of truth.

He spoke of Emerson contemptuously as a scholar and as a speaker.
Speaking of what he called his transcendentalism, and his idea of perfection, or of perfect happiness, ecstasy, which he [Geikie] says was
something about a Hindo without thought," looking at the point of his
nose ;" and a knowledge of which he [Emerson] got by referring to
some translation from the Hindoo language ; all of which is said apparently for the sake of an opportunity to insinuate that whatever ideas
Emerson got from other languages, were got only through translations ;
and in reference to this deficiency, he ends by bringing in the words,
the "American scholar," in such a manner as to try to show that the
world which called him the "scholar," was under a mistake. [We
have to go a roundabout way sometimes for his idea, having but the
report of the *Globe* to help our memory.] True, Emerson in his lecture
did not—to show he understood them—mix in any inelegant quotations
of Latin or French, as did the "scholar" Geikie, but instead of this
shewing the want of a knowledge of them, or of the scholar, it would
rather lead us to the opposite conclusion, since we have been taught
that to stick in a word, or petty phrase of Latin, or any other foreign
language, where the English will do as well or better, is inelegant.
And after something that he had thought compared favourably with
Emerson—perhaps his *own* eloquence, heightened by his Latin and
French—says, "slow speaking Emerson." He appeared to be em-
bued with an "any way, any where" sort of a spirit, but to lower Emerson in the estimation of the people.

He continues contrasting Emerson's doctrines with Christianity,
appearing to think *his* bare mentioning of Emerson's ideas as objectionable or "horrible," a sufficient proof that they are so.

He says, "culture with him is to bring about the reign of the good
and the true. It is to quicken the sensibilities, and fit for that intu-
itive insight which perceives the highest truths," &c. And is this
not culture ? Is it not even the best, the purest, the highest spiritual
culture ? Yet he quotes it as being objectionable, and what he contrasts

with it of Christianity, to throw it in the shade, is something about its "claiming acceptance by the strength of its proofs." The strength of the proofs of Christianity! We think we can partly understand Emerson when he tells us to find the "riches of poverty, the height of lowliness," but when strength of rottenness is spoken of, we wholly fail in understanding what is meant. We have *tried* this proof you call strong, and find it very weakness. It cannot bear up investigation. It wont bear thought. Bring a little general information and reason before it, and it vanishes into smoke, ceases to be a reality. "Philosophy, he says, "never raised either a nation or a tribe." We suppose he embodies, of course, civilization in philosophy—philosophy being the highest step in, or highest result of civilization. What was it raised the Assyrians, the Persians, raised Babylon, the Egyptians, the Greeks, the Romans, the Chinese, &c.? Or what has raised any of even the Christian nations? We deny its being Christianity. Christianity only helps where civilization precedes, or goes with it, and does most. The most that can be claimed for it is that it has helped; but we have undeniable proofs that nations do rise without it, and may remain; in barbarism with it, witness the Abyssinians in Africa, who have been *much* longer in possession of it than the Anglo-Saxons.

About the time Christianity got a full ascendency in Rome, she fell, and the world was engulfed in darkness under the sway of Christianity until printing was invented and ancient *philosophy* revived. [But Mr. Geikie don't let these astounding facts kill you quite, there is more hope of you yet than of a dozen dead men, keep breathing, and you may yet loose the scales from your eyes, though they have been so shamefully plastered over in your youth, and so as to be *likely* to prevent your clear-seeing all your life in this state.] So that his statement that "Christianity leads the savage from ferocity and degradation, to a life of gentleness, honor and love," is not *quite true*. He may tell long yarns at their missionary meetings, to this effect, when they are after the dimes, and be believed by those who never look for facts for themselves, or who shut their eyes against them when they stare them in the face, such as the example of the aborigines of this country affords. We have seen them (the Indians) in their villages, in their houses, in their churches, [or at least those built for them,] where their missionary is supported in idleness, and have found them in the grossest "degradation;" seen them changed from manly independence and freedom, to a state of whining dependency and slavish beggary. Yes, beggary, that corroding disgrace to any nation or people, is one of christianity's handmaidens. We know there are isolated instances, where our Indians have become quite different from this, but it has been owing to their being surrounded by civilization, and kept constantly in contact with it, and having become wealthy from the sale of lands.

Christianity has persecuted and murdered its millions. Behold! the wars between the Unitarians and Trinitarians; the massacre of Protestants by the Roman Catholics in France, where the streets were flooded with the blood of a brother, a sister, or mother, shed by the hand of a brother, a son. Behold the murdering and awful persecutions of the poor Jews!—until civilization checked the rage—a persecution more dreadful, more fiendlike, more unrelenting, perhaps, than any other to be found in the annals of history. Behold the innocent thousands who have been burned for witch-craft! in short, the continuous line of intrigues, cruelty, and bloodshed, kept up by the sects and parties among its devotees; kept up from the commencement of the dark ages, down, down, mournfully, awfully, to the present time. And *now* it is like a mammoth rotten carrion; but, thank God, like it mouldering away, and will shortly, as such, be seen no more; but its elements will be utilized, and, instead of its material grossness, we will have something refined and spiritual, which the good and pure of earth are demanding.

He says Emerson's God is such as has "no bond of sympathy with his creatures, so as to attract their love, &c." But what have we seen in regard to Emerson's love? and we are informed that in his contemplation of God in nature—and which he showed in his lectures—he enjoys the most rapturous delight, and that the "bond of sympathy" is so strong that he feels they are a part and parcel of each other, and his doctrine of the adaptation of one thing to the other, as shown in his lecture, but particularly as quoted by McLachlin, is most beautiful. He says, Emerson "never thinks of directing us to his conception of God for hope," &c., but says, "Christianity tells us that Jehovah is the Father of mercies." Well, which is the superior doctrine? Emerson's. It tells us our hope, and only hope, is in goodness, righteousness, in doing no wrong. Geikie's christianity, that we *may* commit sins of all hues and degrees [except one they call "sinning against the Holy Ghost," but which they cannot explain,] and continue them all our lives—except a few of the last moments—and yet have them all forgiven in a moment, "and remembered against us no more." Emerson's tells us, that for every wrong we do we will receive a proportional punishment. Geikie's, we may commit the wrong but have it immediately forgiven, commit another and with the same result, and so *on*. Which, we ask, will have the greater tendency to cause people to cease sinning. The one is justice, the other injustice. The one is taught on every page of the great book of Nature, so clearly that the most ignorant—the Bushmen, the cannibal—aye, even the dumb brute has a conception of it. The other by a cunning and designing priesthood—consisting of the most stupendous company of speculators known in the history of the world, and believed in by the most wicked, and who allow themselves to be so far duped as to pay in sums of gold to these very priests, for this *mercy*, who, of course pretend to be in league with Geikie's "Father of mercies,"—rather a respectable firm with such a head. He says, this Jehovah is the God of all consolation, but did not point us to any one who appears to have greater consolation than Emerson. Emerson's admiration of the tiny flower, the majestic forest, the singing bird, the adaptation of all things; and his love of *everything*, show his consolation to be perfect. The conviction that Justice reigns is what gives consolation. Geikie's theory after encouraging [indirectly] in sin, may give a hope to the wretched sinner, that he will not have justice dealt out to him. The man who believes all will be right: all is law, order, justice ; of all men he must be the most consolate, for whether he believes in one God, or that three is one and one is three, or in no God, or in many gods and devils, he has a *trust* that *says, whatever* may befall you at "dessolution," will be for the best. If he should feel a desire to live on, or feel confident it would be best that he should retain his individuality after the change, he will be consoled in his belief that he will. Well doing gives consolation. He says, "in the craving in all countries after a personal God, lies a refutation of Pantheism." This assertion amounts to nothing, for the real origin of a belief in a god or gods lies in the deification of *causes ;* the result of the workings of the intellect, as is Pantheism. The former, a conclusion arrived at by the human mind in its infant state of barbarism, the latter by it, in its most cultivated and advanced stages. It may be remarked the one personal God belief is the result of a middle state. How this changes the picture. To see these are facts, behold the men who believe and teach the latter; and look at history, or through your own knowledge of human nature, for the origin of the other. Man's thought, man's attention was first attracted by, and first given to the consideration of the phenomena of nature, which he saw *everywhere ;* and his first sublime thought and question—which stamped *humanity* upon his brow, and which was echoed and re-echoed by the vaults of Heaven, until it resounded through the vast realms of the universe—was, *why?* What's the cause? Yet from all this boundless domain no answer returned, nor will there ever, absolutely speaking; but man has since discovered the relative case. Man never will discover or learn even one, or but one absolute truth. But it was a law of his mental constitution to refer them to causes ; these causes 'hey clothed with personality, and conscious existentence, that willed and acted for themselves, and produced these phenomena. They deified them, and filled the world with demigods and gods.

Geikie manifests, in some of his statements, glaring ignorance, and in his conclusions a great lack of logic, or honesty, or both. But he says in connection with the foregoing; "and in the perfect counterpart to every want of the spirit presented in the Revelation of Jehovah, lies a sufficient vindication of the Scriptures." If this be true, why do men of thought—the best men, the greatest men, the most advanced spirits, say they cannot find the want of the " spirit" there, and seek elsewhere for it, and say they find it? Even *we* feel and know this statement not to be correct. His Revelation and his Scriptures must be the same thing with him, and, if so, makes his argument stand like this : the Bible is divine, because the Bible says so; [which is the almost universal mode of argument used by its defenders as such ; yet the Bible *don't* say so;] but in the formation of his sentence he places them so that the one appears distinct from the other; perhaps this is to give the *appearance* of argument. If he had reversed his statement thus "to the want of *any* spirit" he would have expressed much truth ; the multifarious forms of belief and creeds, the virtues and the vices, that this so-called Revelation of Jehovah countenances, testify to its capability of doing so. The good spirit that loves, may quote its authority, but so do the bad ; the spirit that would rob his fellowman of his liberty—his all—goes there too for its " want :" and fires have been kindled in a thousand piles, by this use made of it, in which human souls have been cast, and the quivering flesh burned from their bones, and their bones to ashes.

He says that Emerson's theology is, that "man is to himself, law, savour, &c.;" and why should it not be a part of it ? it is truth. What *is* law to man, if he is not law to himself ; is it the law of Angels? No ; for in as much as they are not the same as we are ; *their* laws are not appropriate for us, on the same principle that the law of a sheep is not the law of a lion, and in presuming the law of sheep to be the law of lions, we notice the result thus : first, the nature of the lion would be gone, annihilated, the result of this, that he would no longer exist, be, for he could no longer devour his prey, nor even kill it, or catch it, nor could he eat grass, or ruminate ; but, in as much as they are both alike, as both require air to breathe, and food to eat, &c., the law of the one is the law of the other, so in the other case. This clearly demonstrates that man must be a law to himself, or cease to be *man*, [of course, the higher the being the higher the law.] Then if the law of angels is a little too high, on the whole, for man, how stupidly absurd it is to say that the law of God is that of man, or to man. So only in as much as the one is like the other, are the laws of the one the laws of the other. MAN CAN ONLY BE INFLUENCED OR GUIDED BY WHAT MAN CAN CONCEIVE TO BE THE HIGHEST GOOD, and it is a law of his being to seek it. But all beings, all species of existances, on any particular plane, or degree of development, may be influenced—inspired, by those, on the plane above, and *is*, ever has been, and ever will be. It is on the same principle that the better class of society imbues the other with a helping influence or that one individual may another, but unless the communication be such as that the lower can appreciate—except that it be only so far in advance of his own views, or conception, as to link in with them, as it were, or strike him as if he had almost arrived at it himself before, or be in some degree apparent to him—it will be as useless to him as Geikie's latin to a goose. This helps us to see better the beauty and truthfulness of Emerson's saying : "The good reader makes the good book," &c. Reader, this is the great developing principle. The higher, universally throughout Nature, is ever attracting the lower, onward and upward, until the *individual* is perfected. Then, that spiritualism is true [if there are spirits,] there is no table-rapping, horn blowing, or music playing, required to convince those who understand this law, but, to many, they *are* highly necessary. Man is progressive, he inevitably grows from barbarism to civilization. He is a law to himself; he has a conception of the principle of right in his most barbarous state, which becomes more and more developed and refined, until to him virtue becomes its own reward,—until he rises above the plane of approbativeness, where Emerson directs, or leads, when he says: " We should do that with respect to the *excellence* of the work and not its *acceptance ;*" or ascends, till, to him, to give is to receive, than which we can appreciate nothing higher, as yet. This appears the highest point of human perfection. And so it may be said, he is his own saviour, if, indeed, the word can be used with any meaning, or it may be, applied in reference to that gentle hinting—gentle inspiration, or drawing upwards, by the spheres above us, if it must be used.

This inspiration—gentle teaching, or wafting us away to brighter climes or clearer day, is influencing all, but the worst least, and the best most. The wider we open our hearts the more we will receive, and it may be, if we add to our willingness a desire [which is the only kind of prayer but what is absurd] it will still be increased, as it respects from spiritual spheres or plains, but not as it respects the great Posative mind—the fountain of all spirit—God ; for this is the life and the light of all things alike, and to receive more and more is *but* to open wider and wider our hearts ; open our souls for the reception of love, and it will come in and sup with us." This is the fountain from which Emerson has drunk so copiously, that—as Geikie would make out—he has almost mistaken himself for the fountain itself. But Emerson, from what we know of him—we have not read his works—appears to be ignorant of the other source, and does not believe in the *existance* of the spirits, or at least does not teach it. Yet, in our belief he is greatly influenced by them.

Speaking of prayer carries us to Geikie's comparison in the last end of his hunt—hunt, we say, because it reminds us of a hound with his rudder cut off, so that he runs against the trees, &c., and, after *something,* he thinks, but does not know what,—this comparison is between the publican's prayer and some conception of his own, of man in a "dignified," or the loftiest position, declaring the prayer the grander and the nobler; and, as it *is*, it is simply ridiculous. But if he had compared the publican in the act of prayer, to these, we would say there appears a slight shade of contradiction in terms, when we consider his idea, or, his school's idea of prayer, for we have often heard them talk of " *humbling* themselves in prayer," and, in their prayer, tell their God that they " *now* humble themselves before" him, &c.

But, according to Geikie's comparison, when they pray they ought to say, "we now dignify ourselves before thee."

He says Emerson "preaches fate," "Christianity whispers providence." If he would have defined what he meant by providence, &c., there would have been more substance and less of mere shadow in his lecture. He proceeds, like a school boy at play, with a hop, skip, and a jump, and we will not pretend to follow him through all his ramblings. The reader will notice that many of his statements imbody the same meaning as others, and that the refutation of one sometimes, in effect, refutes others, so that we will not dwell upon all of these separately. Fate, in a sense, is preached by everybody. It is the fate of this earth to be, and to be inhabited by living beings, or it is the fate of the Universe to be, and though Geikie's school—who always have the scape-goat word "incomprehensible" to ride off on, when they have nothing to support their theory with—may deny this, by saying, God made it and *could* have left it unmade, [trusting their safety to this scape-goat mode of deliverance, when—as the argument is pursued—it is hinted to them that the universe must have always existed, by asking them, how can something be made from nothing?] they must acknowledge, at least, that its God's fate to be. But we don't like the word, it is not necessary to use it, it is not applicable. If he means by it the immutability of the laws of Nature and their results, well may Emerson thunder fate—because he has everything to support him—whilst Geikie may well only *whisper* providence. By Providence we take him to mean, a special interference of some Omnipotent power. This belief originated with, and is the counter part of the God-belief, having its rise and changes *exactly* corresponding to what we have noticed of the other, therefore already, virtually, scattered to the winds; but we may be more explicit. From time immemorial, and by legions perpetrated, people have fancied such an interference a reality. But, sometimes, as seen they had many gods and godeses: god of the wind, god of the seas, god of love, and a god of hell; godes of pleasure, of wisdom, of fire, of mirth, &c., &c., which were omnipotent each in their sphere, and whom they believed to be "providences," that is, they were special to favorites, and could be flattered. They believed their favor could be incurred by prayer, &c., and "by fire on ten thousand alters," consuming human beings as sacrifices. This is Geikie's "Providence," only in a little grosser form. The Jew had advanced to less extravagance in gods, and to a milder sacrifice, or mode of incurring favor. The Christian tinctures this again with Hindo mythology, imported direct. The three Gods in one God, is clearly traceable to the Brahman's trinity: Brahman, Vishnu, and Siva, who are separate, yet one god; and to some legend about a godess laying three eggs, which, when hatched, produced three gods,—the primary origin of both the Brahmans' and Christians' trinity. The Christian has one most "shocking" and "revolting" idea in his system of favoritism, even the sacrificing of

God himself, or a part of him, whose blood is to avail for the sinner.

> "He breaks the power of cancelled sin,
> He sets the prisoner free;
> His blood can make the foulest clean,
> His *blood avails* for me."

> "Arise, my soul, arise; shake off thy guilty fears,
> A *bleeding sacrifice* in your behalf appears."

And, "except ye drink of my blood, and eat my flesh," &c. O, reason! thou light divine! assert thy right, and hurl this monster belief, that stalks thus at noon-day, out of civilization, and back to the realms of darkness from whence it came. But, on the whole, the Christian's mode of incurring favor is much more refined still than the Jews', and which, in fact, has a tincture of philosophy in part of it, but this is not understood by its practitioners. This tincture, however, does not consist in trying to persuade an Omnipotent power to suspend law and order, and perform some special act, but in so far as it influences finite beings like ourselves, but on higher speres, and in opening our souls, when the spirit that is omnipotent will flow in as naturally as air fills a vaccum. So Geikie's " Providence," when placed in contact with an ounce or two of common sense and reason, or philosophy, becomes effervescent. And what a blessing it would be to society, if it were rid of it. The individual groaning with aches, and pains, and sickness, instead of impiously imputing—instead of believing " Providence" the cause, would soon discover the cause to be a violation of fixed laws, and would learn to violate them no more, and that these laws and effects *must* be immutable, or else there would be no order, and if no order, no happiness, no existance; and that, therefore, these penalties or corrections attached to violations, are in reality, for our good, and when he sees this truth and beauty in physical " law and order" he will soon discover the same in the mental or moral. The loving mother, too, would no longer believe a jealous " Providence" murdered her little cherub—her little pet—her little darling—because she loved it too much—because it made her too happy, or because she loved it more than Him, but would learn the cause, and apply the remedy, if she should be blessed with such another care. And the adoring wife, the worshiping husband, would continue to be the spring of each other's joy—the soul of each other's bliss— the life of each other's life; without the fear of exciting the jealousy and anger of a " Providence," who would rob the one of the other, because he was jealous of their loves, but would, on the other hand, believe that the *deeper*, the *higher*, the *greater* their love, the more meritorious.

He says, Emerson "dismisses all responsibility from human acts." What we have just been showing negatives Geikie's " Providence," which he opposes to *this* idea of Emerson's, therefore, this showing is Emerson's view, and is so according to Geikie; but does it do what Geikie has just said? No; but it does the very reverse: it *makes human acts responsible*; then this statement is not correct. He says, he [Emerson] "obliterates the phraseology of right and wrong, obedience and sin." He does not ; but the difference between the two is, one gives them their true meaning, whilst the other's view of them is a bundle of jargon—like this : Once, upon a time, there was a rebellion in heaven ; the leader of the rebellion and his brother rebels met the God of Heaven and the loyalists in battle, but was defeated. and cast into hell, "*prepared* for the devil and his angels" This Devil—the general-in-chief of the rebellion—had got to be proud in his heart, which pride appears to be the first appearance of disobedience and sin, but which subsequently became so dominant that countless millions have been, and are continuing to be "conceived in iniquity and born in sin," and that now *all*—"*all*, are by nature, as prone to sin as sparks are to fly upwards." [But these "shocking" absurdities are so innumerable, we do not undertake to give anything like a logical arrangement of them.] The spirit of right and obedience we have nothing of, and can obtain none of it, except we believe a certain theory—which is impossible for many to believe—and if we do not believe, what is our doom? Behold! Oh behold ! * * * * * * * But since we are wholly "chilldren of the Devil," why should we *not* be "heirs of Hell?" The Devil, who was once an angel of light, is the source and fountain of evil. God the source and fountain of good. Yet God is the origin of all *things*, and yet the Devil, or his essence-evil, pervades all things out of heaven. So Geikie has a Pantheism too, but verily it "hath a devil." Let the reader reflect upon the many questions which suggest themselves to the mind, in looking at these things, which we have not time or space to notice. But Emerson's idea of right and wro. g is that they are relative terms, the same as heat and cold, light and darkness, none of which are *absolu'e* realities, but are *relative* realities, that is, without cold there would be no heat—without heat no cold. Compared with *this*, *that* is cold, compared with *that*, *this* is hot. Just so with right and wrong. Then, in the sense that we are free agents,—and we are free agents only in a relative sense,—we may do either right or wrong. The "Relative Theory" explains this more fully. Nor is there either reward or punishment, in a proper light, but simply if we obey the laws we will be happy, if not we cannot be. There is chastisement attached to the violation of law, that we may learn the law—learn what we should do, and what we should not do. The higher the law by which any being is governed, the greater that being's chance of happiness—and, we might say, of unhappiness,—and the more we obey the higher laws, the more we are preparing ourselves for still higher—the more we are becoming capacitated for happiness.

After being up into these regions of loveliness it is painful to descend to Geikie's cramped theory, for when one is dealing with a ridiculous thing and ridiculous actions, he has to descend to ridicule, more or less ; and when one is dealing with error and dishonesty, the more he

hates dishonesty the more likely he is to become sarcastic and severe ;
then let these considerations —and perhaps a little desire to be mirth-
ful—be our excuse for manifesting or using these occasionlly as we do.
If we had had honesty and error to do with, and had descended to
ridicule or severity, we would have been unpardonable. But to our
task. He says, " In life we may dream our theories, but death is the
experiment that proves their worth." This is a grand mistake—or a
stupid on—or else Paganism ' as been proved right by a million deaths ;
human sacrifices by a million devotees, and the hundred forms of religion—from the darkest Paganism to the " Harmonial Philosophy"—
all right, by the deaths of countless millions. He quotes from a
dying Pantheist these words : " certainly he had none, and has nothing
for it, but to keep shut the lid of those secrets." Well, this says but
liltle, surely, but we may gather from it that the man doubted something, but whether it was what he had believed, or something his system
had not extended to or pretended to, settle, we cannot discover. In
saying, all he had for " certainly" was to *do* something, is certainly
childish talk. The quoting, "to keep shut the lid of these secrets,"
appears to be intended to show an article of their faith. We don't
know what the belief of Pantheists is about after death, but there
don't appear to be much sense in what is quoted, and less in the
quoting of it. And then he talks about "poor human bravery, that ties
to keep down the lid of the future." Who ever heard of any one
doing this ? Why, all are anxious to try to raise the lid. Man has
ever had a desire to look *into* the future. But there are wise and good
men, who do not believe there is a future, and of course they don't
try to keep down the lid of what *is not*. No one, then, will wish the
lid of the future kept down, except he dreads it, and no one dreads it
except he believes in a false doctrine, and such an one as requires a
compliance with rules, &c., and which rules he has not complied with;
but to apply the word bravery to this act looks like something unnatural—like a language monster. He says, "compare its [Pantheism's]
darkness and unspeakable sadness with the Christian's vision of the future, ; which vision he then quotes from Bunyan's novel. But what
has he quoted or said, that warrants him in applying such epithets to
Emerson's doctrines ?—we say nothing. But to make assertions and to
not prove, or even to try to substanciate them, were prominent characteristics of his lecture, though, a contravertial lecture. Evidently, these
phrases are used on the same principle, as all his school apply the
words Infidel &c., to those whose arguments they cannot answer. The
picture of immortality in Giekie's theory is one thing we like better
than what appears to be Emerson's view on that point. He says "the
best and the worst in his [Emerson's] eyes are the same." Not so,
for no one exercising his senses would say *two* things are the same
thing, he might say the two are parts of a same *one* ; but if he meant
that in Emerson's eyes, they are equally respectable and lovely ; by
considering Emerson's own statements in his lecture, we will see it

contradicted: for after enumerating a list of noble arts and useful feats he says, "these are arts to be thankful for, and we could not chose but respect them." This certainly implies that if they were arts, worthless or bad, he could chose to not respect them. And why should he labour to teach us to change from worse to better, and how to become good, and great, or successful, and condemn the practice of making ourselves appear great by "exclusion," by "egotism," by hurrah and bragg." [one might think he had been acquainted with Geikie hearing him refer to these.] He told us "Nature utilises misers, fanatics, &c., but that we must not think the better of them for that." Giekie says, "Christi..nity has the response of our bosoms in hanging up a deathless crown before him who seeks after righteousness." This may have the "response" of Giekie's heart no doubt, but compared to what Emerson taught—"We should do that with respect to the *excellence* of the work and *not* its *acceptableness*,"—it is low, mean, it is like holding out a lump of sugar to a spoiled child.

What cultivated mind does not at once see the greatness, and agree to Emerson's rule, yet in reality it condemns what Geikie's heart responds to, and what he says Christianity does. He says, "Pautheism scoffs at the idea of mediation" ; and well it might, for it is absurd in the sense that Christians use it. The only sense in which it is possible, is between us and other finite beings—angels and men, and between man and man &c., But he says, "hnmanity by the fire or ten thoualters craves it, and Christianity offers it." These fires and alters—though we may not have used these words—we have shewn to be a mode of worship, or efforts to gain favour direct from the gods, or God, and has no reference to mediation. He says Emerson "offers no code, no rule for our guidance towards God and our neighbour." We only need to quote still again, that great principle and rule, to prove this statement wrong, and defy Giekie to offer a "code, or rules of action" either "towards God or our neighbour," superior to it. Though he imbodies with the thirty and nine *articles,* all the creeds, and codes, and rules of all the sects, we think he will come short of it —To think and act, "with the respect to the *excellence*" of the thought or deed, &c. But the idea of a code of rules for our guidance towards God, is rediculous in the extreme. There is a code of *perfect* laws, [and therefore ought to be, and are immutable,] for our guidance to happyness, and if we violate them, it is our own business, we alone are responsable. God neither rewards or condemns us. But these matters—mediation &c.—are of not much consequence to these men, [Emerson &c.] as touching themselves, because they are happy with or without the belief— being reconciled— being convinced, to be good is to live *well* -- is to live aright —to live aright is to be happy.

They are above the plane of reward, which looks to them like being hired to live well. To them "virture is its own reward." He says, "It

is a striking enforcement of humility, to find modern philosophy, to fail
so utterly in its efforts, to make a religion for itself." "So utterly!"
Now this eloquent sentence is a mere bubble—"sounding brass or
tinkling symbol," for we can speak for ourselves and say,—taking the
word to mean a system of belief which satisfies ones self, and attracts
people to it—it has *not failed* ; and according to what we have seen and
heard, there are millions who can say the same : and the increase
has been—in the last few years—more rapid than that of any sectarianism under the Heavens, and is now increasing more rapidly than before. And according to this assertion "modern philosophy" has failed
to do what all degrees and shades of knowledge and intelligences,
down to the darkest state of Heathemism, have succeeding in doing,—
for all these "have made a religion for themselves"—and humbled
itself beneath all these. But having a *religion* merely, is no great
criterion of merit, or mark of goodness, look at Christianity for instance ;
and there are still worse. There are religionists in India who appease
their God by robbery and murder ; but you may say, so do christians, in
their burning heretics, &c., but we mean these others make a profession
of it.

But to take the word [religion] in one sense, and we need none, and
in an other, it is not a thing to be male at all.

He says it would be well for Emerson to believe "that human wisdom is worth little or nothing." Ah, Mr. Emerson stop, where you
are ! drop your studies ! take no more delight in feeding the hungry for
wisdom, for it is "worth little or nothing" to them ; their desire is a
mock, their love for wisdom a phantom, your efforts a farce.—
Thou hast spent thy life unprofitably—foolishly all—the joy, the
happiness, that thou hast reaped from wisdoms ways, has been a
shadowy dream. And you savans, philosophers, teachers, students,
all, cease to fret your fevered brain, your wisdom will not be worth the
oil you burn, it hath never made you happy nor will it ever. Burn your
libraries, convert your univers ties into priest's, temples, and invite
Geikie to preach to you from "Human wisdom is worth little or nothing." But hold ! perhaps he is not honest, he has not burned his own
books yet !

And what sort of wisdom does he consider woith something,
is it that of a pig, or a sheep ? or is it that of Angels, or God ?
it cannot be the latter, for their wisdow can be of no use to us, but as
we can appreciate it—understand it—and in as much as we can understand it, it *is human* wisdom.

He says, "better than the &c. "is the trust of the veriest babe or
suckling, (he ought to have said nursling before the ladies) in whom
God has perfected praise." We have said there was an idea given
by Emerson we could not fully appreciate ; well, in this one parti-

cular, this last quoted of Geikie's stands the same. He has gone beyond our comprehension, but the difference is, the *sublimity* of the one, and the *rediculousness* of the other. But no doubt he thought he was saying something.

But Mr. Giekie's lecture was eloquent, and bespoke for its author, considerable brilliancy of immagination, and a happy stye of communication. Yet it may be thus characterized.Much, presumption,—little sense,—less argument.

Mr. Giekie appears a victim of the cramming system of education, and hence, though he may possess the learning of the schools, has a broken constitution, a dwarfed mind, and is without. *that* which scholastic education is only a means—a help to get. He has the seed grain but not the crop, and is trammeled in the meshes of sectarianism;—whilst Emerson's case is nearly a reversal of this picture. He has "valued his talents as it is a door into nature," and has reaped a harvest—has regaled himself with nature's fragrances;—now, listening with attentive ear and grateful soul to her lessons of wisdom ; now, basking in her genial sunshine ; now, reclining in her shady bowers listening to her songs of melody and gazing with ecstacy upon her chequered beauties, and ever drinking from her inexhaustible fountains of wisdom and truth. He is bound by no bands of superstition or bigotry, he is a freeman, and his great soul extends the hand of fellowship, and love, to all mankind; whilst Giekie *donounces* all who do not come within the pale of his narrow creed,—Emerson is original and spiritual, Giekie an imitator and material. Emerson's doctrines the want of the age, Giekie's, a superstitious relic of the past. Emerson a great shining light of himself, like the sun, Giekie like the moon, reflects a borrowed glimmer, which, when Emerson crosses our horizon, is no longer even visible—sinks to a nothingness.

Out of the dark ages civilization emerged thus. Germany first, France next, Britain next, America will be next ; and exactly cor. responding to this has been, and are the religious casts.

The philosophy of Germany long ago superseded her sectarianism, and is now the most profound in the world, and is represented by Goethe. The philosophy of France has done the same for her except perhaps as it regards the women—and is represented socially, and theologically by Furrier. The philosophy of Britain has not done so much for her yet, but is rapidly effecting it, and is represented by Carlyle. America's case is peculiar. Leaving out spiritualism, her case is nearly the same as Britain's. Her philosophy and religious element, represented by Emerson. But taking spiritualism into account, she may even now be considered in advance of the rest of the world. It has been said that Emerson as a writer on the whole, is perhaps the greatest in the present age. But there is a man called

Andrew Jackson Davis, who may be said to be favoured above any other living personage. He appears to belong, to some degree, to both this and the spiritual world. He appears to be suspended between the two. He is only sometimes Davis, at others he is an instrument, a medium for the transmission of angelic thought and wisdom to us, at others he appears to ascend into Heaven and bring back showers of briliant gems. But even when he is Davis his soul is unfathomable, for he retains much of these visions. He had no scholastic education, yet his works are volumnious, and perhaps excel all others. He is *the* phenomenon of the age.

But "oh my country!" Our dear native Canada what shall we say for thee. Why hast thou not kept pace with thy neighbour. Thou hadst as majestic forests, as beautiful a sky, as sublime scenery to inspire thy sons as any—yet thou art priest riden. No Tell hath arisen for thy liberty. No philosopher to purify thy morals. No lover of Nature to reflect her precepts. No great heart that hath burst into freedom, and spoken from its fulness. The nearest approach to a great free soul, is McLacklan, and therefore to him we must look as your representative at present. But we will hope. Some of thy younger sons may arise to speak for thee. We are preparing to help. We mourn our inability to help thee now. But we hope !

There is an unhappy land, far, far away,
Where Sepoys and Britains stand, each, to slay ;

which we must not over-look. India that land of all relegions, surely must have *some* good ideas. And when it is considered that some of their people can suspend life, be buried for an indefinite length of time, be resurected, and walk forth hale and hearty, it must be granted that they are acquainted with some of the great laws of our being, which all the rest of the world is ignorant of, and that she is so far superior to all others. There must be much to be admired in their philosophies.

The McLacklan just referred to, is the one before spoken of as having lectured after, and in the same place as Geikie. We refer to this because his subject was partly the same as Geikie's. His lecture was on poets—Hood, Emerson &c. This man shewed a growth, and liberality of soul, that tours far above Mr. Geikie's. There is in him, poetry and philosophy, love and truth. He is *nearly* a freeman. You can see his elbows and knees out—bursting through his swadling clothes—the errors of "early impression." He spoke of Emerson like one who could afford to speak well of a great man, and like one disposed to allow every man his due. But he too must pander a little, to the prejudices of the people. He said Emerson's works should be *read with caution.* This implies there is error ignorantly or willfully propagated, and when he gives us no proof, that there is, he asks us to treat one with distrust without grounds for so doing, which is a slight insult, It

54

too leaves us no means of judging for ourselves, which of the two ought to be *read* with the more *caution.* It shews presumption to expect us to believe his mere say so, when he knows we have reason to believe, that if the other party were present to speak for himself, he would reverse, or deny the justice of the statement. It is too much like the dogmatical cant of ranters.—On this occasion, The Hon. J. H. Cameron presided, and made perhaps the most ridiculous and glaring attempt at popularity of any. After expressing his approbation of the lecture's sentiments, relative to the beauty and use of poetry, he referred us to he Bible, as the fountain of poetry, [more poetry than truth then, thought we,] from the first of Genesis throughout, its pages were lined with poetry, some of which nothing equaled. When he resumed his seat, we were much nearer convinced, that he had never read the Bible than before. We felt bad, for we were disappointed. We had fancied to our selves a well developed soul, looking at him through the medium of his profession. We came away more confirmed in the belief, that ones soul may be developed all on one side, like the handle of a jug, or that one may have a hump-backed mind.—a mind highly cultivated on one side and neglected on the other. What poetry could Mr. Cameron see in the story of Lot and his Daughters, the allusions of Ezekiel, the genealogies, the petty details of petty things, the rapine, the murder committed by the Jews, Samson's killing thirty men to rob them of their garment, with which to pay a *bet* he had lost? or in the shocking accounts of falsehood, deception, wrong &c. &c.? even the worst of which are said to be directed and permitted by God.

True, in our remarks touching Christianity, we have given its dark side. It has a bright side, with many beauties. What can be sweeter in expression, and more pleasing in sentiment than,

"There is a happy land, far, far away,
Where saints in glory stand, bright, bright as day."

And even many of its errors are founded on some degree of philosophy. Its confession's of faults and sins to a superior, either in the Methodist class meeting, or before the priest, has for its foundation the principle and duty of "letting ourselves be known." Its merciful God, and malignant Devil, has for its foundation the fact of the existence of both good and evil, relatively speaking.—Its Eternal happiness, and Eternal misery, for its foundation, the possibility of our partaking of the good, and becoming happy, or of partaking of the evil, and being miserable. Its idea of God's mercy, the charity we ought to have for one-another. Prayer and mediation, upon the psychological sympathy, or dependancy between all finite beings. Its idea of Gods Eternal existence and omnipresence, upon the fact that—"All is but a Unity," "Which ever was will ever be" But these last two look to be the same, for whatever is every where, must be itself everything, since two things cannot occupy the same place at the same time.

We reject Christianity then, not because it hath no light, but because it has so much darkness, and because, in our minds it is superseded by a system, that hath *more* light, and *less* darkness. And as we have said before, we speak more particularly of Christianity, such as it has become, not such as Christ taught. But if you Doctors of Divinity—or Mr. Geikie, who is more bold than you--think you are right, and we are wrong, vindicate the right, and confound the wrong. Give the people an opportunity of judging. If you are silent it will show you do not yourselves, believe you have truth on your side. This you have often shewn, you have been challenged in this City, to meet face to face, by your opponents, but you were mute as mice—as silent as the grave. We are but weak—but a school-boy, studying his grammar—but *truth* is strong. And though by presumption and audacity, you may daunt the boy, and by exhausting your vocabulary of hard names upon him, [which you keep for such purposes,] prejudice the people against him, you may but dread him the more when he grows up. You ought to wake up to something. You are living on the people, but don't give them the worth of the salt in your victuals. Your sermons are like musty ruins, no life, no growth. They are bundles of mysticism and jargon. You tell the people they are rotten with iniquity—putrified sores "from the crown of their heads to the soles of their feet," by nature—and that this has condemned them to * * *— and hence their resemblance to it, for people are *apt* to be what they *think* they *are*. But you flatter them in the meantime, by telling them there is a *way* to escape this doom, and that *you* can let them into the secret —that *you* can teach them the *way*, and that *you* are the *only* ones who teach the *right* way, [no wonder, those believing all this, should give you a fat living.] You say to them, this way is a belief in *somthing* you tell them about. This belief then is a righteous act, since it not only frees them from this condemnation, but as you say too, gains for them eternal bliss. But at another time you tell them they cannot perform a good act, or think a good thought. And your saying, [when you are asked to explain this,] that God influences them, or [which it amounts to] makes them believe, besides showing your doctrines to be a glaring humbug and farce, it destroys the necessity of your teaching, your plea for office, and reduces the matter to this point—and which we believe some have got to-- "God will have mercy on whom he will have mercy," and that therefore our concern and efforts avail nothing towards preventing the one, or securing the other— but some how or other even then you stick to office. Your doctrines are absurd and self-destroying--your interference between your fellow-man and God, a glaring speculation, and your systematized, and organized bodies from the Pope down to your Methodist class-leader, a concocted scheme to carry it out. You have always opposed all reform. You have been deadly enemies to the progress of the sciences. You would now blast he prospects—shut up in dungeons—and burn at the stake (if the civil law did not prevent you) those who would but speak their honest convictions that your doctrines are wrong, and pretend to teach, that to be come good and wise, is to do right and become happy—pretend to teach the people that all wrong doing inevitably brings unhappiness, and well *doing alone* happiness, and that they [the people] need no hired priest to tell them this, for the most ignorant, yea the most bar barous have a conception of it ; that Nature teaches it to *all* her child ren ; and her doctrines never clash ; and though her voice never ceases night nor day, there is no discord, hers is a Harmonious Philosophy, and can teach all that man will ever know, either in *Heaven* or *here-below*.

> " What conscience dictates to be done,
>   Or warns me not to do,
> This teach me more than hell to shun,
>   That more than heaven pursue."

TORONTO, January, 1859.